'The White Cockatoo

On his Eighteenth Birthday Timothy Rogers found out that he was adopted, and that his Parents, as he had thought them, were not in fact his original Parents at all.

The shock of the discovery almost caused him a nervous breakdown. For the first time in his life, on the Eve of his Coming of Age, he had asked for his Birth Certificate so that he could go out drinking Legally with his friends for the first time ever.

When he discovered by it's means that he had been adopted at about the age of three years old, he felt a rush of acute resentment towards his (newly understood to be Adoptive) Parents for not having made him aware of the situation far earlier.

He'd taken the Certificate out of his Dad's hands, and placed it in the inner pocket of his coat without looking at it initially, but he had taken it out again to examine it more closely when he was by himself in the Bathroom. His stomach had sunk on reading it, and he had felt queasily dizzy with absolute outrage.

He put the toilet seat down and sat near the pedastol beneath it, resting his hand on the peach seat itself, and tried to hold back the feeling of dismay and physical wretchedness. After about ten minutes he noticed that his eyes were wet with tears, which he had to brush away before the sobbing started. He did not want his Dad to hear it. He had not yet decided fully what approach might best suit the situation of himself feeling suddenly bereaved from his own identity. He turned the bath tap on in order to conceal the signs of his heartbreak, and taking up the bath mat, which was softly plush, rubbed it for comfort like a Teddy Bear of old against his right cheek.

He wondered whether he would be strong enough to keep his urge to somehow punish his Parents pent up, and buried deep as he might try and act as though everything was still as normal.

His Dad had given him the Certificate without prelude of any discussion or explanation, casually handing it over to him without even bothering to look uncertain about it.

Timothy's adoptive Mother was out of the house that evening as she had taken on a new job answering Emergency Telephone Calls for the Council. She must have surely known that this had been on the cards to happen: that he would need his Birth Certificate to prove his age that night. Was she intending to humiliate him purposely, or make him feel so utterly a fool? She had given him a new Dressing Gown that morning and a couple of pairs of socks as well as announcing that she had put a hundred pounds into his Account. Somehow, she must have set up an Account for him ages ago without he himself having been present: Surely she would have had to have shown his Birth Certificate to do so…? Somehow he had not questioned that a couple of years earlier, when he had started working part-time at the weekend at the Pizza Shop on the corner, and when he had been so busy keeping up with School-work.

It might be thought fairly miraculous, given the times, that Timothy had waited till his Eighteenth Birthday before even thinking about asking for an Alcoholic drink in a Pub: the truth was that he had had quite a few severe hangovers already but at the houses of friends from Sixth Form: it was he himself who had made a big deal about the fact that tonight he could do it Legally (partly because he was resentful about the fact that some people had obviously tried to drag him down, and partly because he so much naturally wanted to be a popular young man amongst his Peers. His Adoptive Dad had caused in him a Numerical form of Dyslexia quite early on. He had never thought before that his Step-Dad might have actually, though behaving so decently on so many occasions, wanted to engineer the thwarting of his chances earlier on.

Maths had played an important part at the School that Timothy had attended, and this Numerical Dyslexia had caused untold humiliation for years and years. The Pizza Job and the drinking sessions had been the only way out of his former unpopularity, it had seemed.

So had his Step-Dad intentionally caused the problem? For all Timothy knew his Step-Parents may have been given large amounts of money for taking him on. For all he knew, he might be one of the Royal Family's Sons.

He took some exaggeratedly deep breaths, and rubbed his chest up and down to try and soothe himself. Did it make sense to ignore the fact, that he had read his Birth Certificate, and to carry on with the rest of the Evening without challenging his Dad to some questions? He meant his Step-Dad, of course.

It was 7.15 pm and he was due to meet Phil and the rest of the party at 8pm, and he had yet to find some new batteries to put in his bike lights. It had been worrying the night before when he had been cycling back from Andy's when his bike had jolted into a pot-hole on a darkish un-street-lit lane, and all the batteries had jolted out as his front light had jumped away from its cradle and crashed to the Tar. At least that had not gone into the ditch, and it had not seemed to be broken either, but as far as the batteries went he could not see them around, although he'd got off his bike to look for a while. He felt threatened not only by cars going faster than they should have been but even also Lorries, presumably making their way to a Local Industrial Estate. He knew he would have to keep off his bike and stumble back later than ever into the early hours of the morning. He had had a few cans, and he found it alarmingly simple to realise that he might be in an even more dangerous situation if he lingered too long to try and look in the grassy area near the ditch for the scattered batteries. It was ludicrous anyway...a bike light needing four AA Batteries...though its short life had been powerful enough to light his way somewhat through the darkened areas it had been too heavy and cumbersome, compared with his old Dynamo, which really had served him well years before Dynamos had been banned. As though it was befitting that Cyclists should have been inconvenienced to suit impatiently intolerant and dangerous car-drivers!

*

It seemed so many years later...It was indeed so many years later, that Timothy found himself wondering whether to risk taking his own young Son Eriquet to Flamingo Land.

The Numerical Dyslexia had caused a great deal of trouble in so many ways socially and academically, but even still he had magical Dreams of the White Cockatoo.

It had played its part on numerous visits, and never tired him even though it somewhat perplexed him, alongside a Grey-Blue Parrot and a Green and Red Parrot, both of which could also talk quite understandably, and had always finished up the Routine taking Centre Stage so many years ago.

All of them had been able to count, and Timothy could have sworn, could still believe indeed, that there had been less trickery and more Animal Magic attached to the Show than most of the Newspapers would have admitted credible.

If the wizened old Bird-Trainer asked the three Birds to tap their beaks on the wood beneath them, or to pat their clawed feet on the stands in response to the numbers he held up to be translated into Action, the three of them would get it absolutely, without uncertainty, right. Then the large cards would be shuffled and they would guess accurately which card it was going to be. A Member of the Audience would pick a random card and they would still guess accurately, much to all of the Audience's surprise. Then they would be asked to make as good an estimate as they could as to how many people there were in fact forming the audience, from which people could join or drift away if they were pressed for time….and it certainly seemed to those counting hairstyles rather than sheep dreamingly, that they might have plucked the right number without doubt.

One time Timothy himself had been recruited up from the Audience to choose which of the Numbers to ask the Birds to tap or beat with their feet, and he was invited on purpose to try and perplex them as much as he could. At first he had eased them in by choosing a number seven, and then when they got that right he had taken both a number 2 and a number 4 and put them side by side, wondering when he switched the order around whether they would tap twenty-four or even forty-two times. All three of them had tapped in perfect synchronisation six times in each case, the entire six with their left foot when it was twenty-four, and four with their right feet and two with their left when it was forty-two, with a very-slight, almost undiscernible pause between the two linking the sequence. He thought that the birds might have possibly been trained to read from left to right in numbers as humans were in most domains, though he had wondered whether that custom differed regionally ever.

And he had blamed his Step-Dad? When there had even been ice-creams afterwards?

Did Timothy dare to risk giving his own Son the same complex that had been responsible both for his Social Subjection, but also for the wonderful Dreams and an unwavering attachment to Birds and Animals, and strong belief in their significant intelligence?

Another time he had visited Flamingo Land and it really had amazed him almost as much, because there really had been Flocks upon Flocks of Flamingos visible: so many that he could not hope to count them very well at all. Some people might find that difficult to believe now, but his Step-Dad, who had moved to Switzerland, would still have the Photographs.

Somehow the Park had seemed a lot bigger that time, and almost inescapable, and there had been a multiplicity of Lake Areas...all filled up with pink and white Flamingos fishing against the Sunsetting behind them and mirroring into the Lakes, some stood up with one foot bent, others more swan-seeming-like. In fact the Park had got so much bigger that his Step-Parents could not easily find their way in the car to the main Exit onto the main road, and it really did take more than half-an-hour before the Natural Labyrinth was shirked off from their start at the Car-Parking area.

*

Timothy was worried that his Partner Jennifer would think that he was having some kind of mid-life Crisis if he mentioned too much the possibility (which he worried may not in any way be possible) of a change of Career. He had been fortunate enough to have been taken on and kept successfully for years as a Photographer for an Estate-Agents, but he still felt not only a wavering impulse, but increasingly a compulsion to try and be a Wildlife Photographer for a Magazine. However, he had looked into the matter, and was not convinced that any Magazines were currently rich enough to pay even for a meagre contribution.

He had found himself increasingly having to use self-hypnosis techniques at work to prevent himself from running away literally form the desk, and Jennifer really thought he ought, and he often thought it so too, to be grateful to sit in the not-too-draughty back area of the Shop at a smart-enough desk, with occasional need for on-site visits in his smart Beige Peugeot.

The White Cockatoo had been a Master of Ceremonies at presenting Optical-Illusion Puzzles, such as bent coloured Rainbow-shapes over-and-under that seemed differing lengths, but were proved, by its using a piece of purple wool, to be the same exact length. Proved by the agile techniques the White Cockatoo was supremely capable of. The routine had been awe-inspiring as well as somewhat disconcerting.

Daily now, the White Cockatoo visited his woken consciousness as he tried to dream his way away from Elspeth, Brandon and Parry as they swapped lurid stories in the Office that he preferred not to be tricked by.

Sometimes it seemed more blazingly white than others, depending on the lack of shadow; at others more cream or even sometimes yellow.

But when it opened its wings and showed every curve of its main flying feathers it was astonishingly, undoubtedly, radiant in every specially remarkable way.

Some people were wanting to be believed that Rainbows themselves are in fact Optical Illusions, but that would entail not merely a folie-a-deux, but a trick to hundreds of witnesses....and beside that, Timothy did not necessarily think that explaining it away as a mere Illusion may be an adequate response.

People generally made out that aspects of the Atmosphere we breathe in are invisible completely, but that invisibility must accumulate somehow into having become an absolutely visible factor, undeniable and present-to-behold in the Cloud-formations daily, and, yes, he had seen shapes of the White Cockatoo displayed to him way above, and the Mountains of Scotland many times as well.

Lately Timothy had heard of disputes at Kirkby-Misperton over Fracking, and that had worried his peace-of-mind still further. So much so, it was like being threatened by unnecessary brain-surgery.

If Fracking was common in the U.S. of A. what had led to that being the case? More Cowboy Lawless Entrepreneurs? Phil had used to joke about Joan Collins in Dallas being his Father's version of J.C. In some ways, in many ways, it was not at all that funny. What had happened to Oil Production in Texas if there was a need for Fracking there now at all? Or was it just that they had no sense of the Common-good?

Sometimes he even suspected Fracking might have been secretly continued at some sites in England despite the Government's laudable attempts to outlaw it, unbeknownst to most members of the Public, and that that might be one of the main reasons for the polluted water of some of the Rivers. He could only hope that that was not the case, and that members of his own Generation had not been led-astray so much as to have used up all the available energy-source.

He had never had that conversation with his Step-Dad, and had never found out who his original Parents were. His Step-Dad had never mentioned the missing batteries. Sometimes he wondered tentatively whether he might be a Twin, or even a Triplet.

Watching a flock of Swallows fly past he also wondered whether they were feeling glad to have returned to England, and what they would think on their arrival back home, if the same Trees they had lodged in a Season ago might still certainly exist.

Most often there were no Birds on House Photographs, not even in the 'extensive Back Garden'. Mot perched on the Roof, or the Arial, or Telephone Wire. Maybe he might change that now. Most of them wanted almost a Guarantee that white bird droppings would not be a problem on recently-fitted slate roofs, nor would any of them want the hazard of birds getting in the way of backing-out of their Drive-ways.

Maybe Flamingo-Land would still have a Relative of the same White Cockatoo entertaining if they could still afford to keep up with paying a good patient Trainer. He worried that so much of the old magic might be inaccessible nowadays, He would not want to depress his Son, nor force him to risk a formidably frightening Fairground Ride instead of witnessing an Animal Intelligence Marvel, if the White Cockatoo was no longer represented.

The White Cockatoo had haunted Timothy somewhat in its surreal absolute intelligence, but he dreaded the experience of finding out that the Bird Show might have been cut….there had surely not been any cruelty attached to it…..so much that he kept delaying having the certainty p0laced on the hypothesis, and instead he tried to teach Eriquet too to use Sky-watching as an Escape.

Soon, he would also train him to Self-Hypnotise, and would hope that that way somehow what was looking like it might be an every-inwardly closing Prism situation might nevertheless prove to be something dodged out-from.

"Look at that wonderful Lake!" he pointed up, glad that his Son did have the experience of being able to be in the company sometimes of his own true Father, but no longer angry with his Step-Dad, who still gave him a Telephone call every fortnight from the Swiss Library, which he managed.

Sometimes the Clouds looked doom-laden and gloomy, but most often they seemed to still promise hope for imagination and reality.

'Crazy Golf'

Dixon was undoubtedly extraordinarily good at Crazy Golf. When the family visited Southport he excelled his own reckonings even further than usual, and even got a hole-in-five on the most difficult test at the end of the run, which was set up not only with the encounter of a rotating Windmill, but also a clockwork mouse that needed to be wound up before the start of the exercise, and that ran up and down the Windmill at the back of the sails, trying once more to dislodge the Player into a state of frustration even in the half-second spaces between the Windmill sail-turns. And another Mouse on exit, that kept trying to dodge the ball off course later on, nosing around from side to side at an angle and swivelling fully to try and bar the ball eventually from attaining the final hole-slot, like a crazed rodent Goal-keeper.

The air had been so salty by the sea you could taste it on your palate.

It had been very late August and the nights were drawing in again. Margerie was with them (she had been friends with Dixon's Nanna before his Nanna had died) and was rumoured to be a very rich woman, though all she talked about that night was not the fun that riches could bring, but the worry that she would soon be packed off into a Nursing Home and all her Property File taken off her. She frightened him terribly by explaining in drawn out sherry-trickled slurs, that especially for an older woman, and even and even particularly a rich old woman, it only took one enemy who might spread a false report for the Council to take steps to storm in and destroy what remained of her life completely.

Dixon tried not to believe her. He wanted to be a Policeman like his Uncle. He wanted to be able to believe that if he chased someone into a hole, like his aim had been so accurate even on the toughest stage of Crazy Golf, it would be a villain indeed that had needed chasing and putting inside.

Otherwise, he would have Nightmares, being not a massively chunky toughened-up boy, that maybe he was too vulnerable to be able to voice up his own cause should he be threatened, and press for the benign help of the Justice System.

Lately he had also been bothered by fringe-Nightmares of people fighting in Films, and loudened voices, and limbs flying about angrily in all directions with the intentions of causing harm for no other reason than to display power.

He hadn't been able to eat the Evening Meal at the Guest House that night, even though he had been hungry after the Golf and playing about all day with the bucket and spade…it had seemed too much literally like codswallop. And his Dad had been angry with him for embarrassing him by saying so loudly, and his Sister had even pulled his hair again from behind, more than a tug, and he would indeed have been miserable if it hadn't been for the fact that another Family in the Family Entertainment Room were playing cards nicely. The girl had a pretty dress on and looked neat with bunches in blue ribbons. Sometimes they laughed, in a natural-sounding way, not at all as though they had been paid to sound happy.

But then Margerie did an extraordinary thing, and offered to pay for him to have a Supper later of Bread-and-Butter Pudding, complete, probably, with Sultanas and Raisins, and maybe even a sprinkling of Cinnamon. And warmish Custard, which would have cooled into being thicker and more sugary than when it had first been served up.

Graciously, he accepted the invitation, quite enthusiastically.

But just as the Waitress was bringing it into the area which really had not been designated for eating in, his Dad re-entered from the Bar next door, and caught on to what was going on. And it really had been true, truer than it had ever been, that Dixon was still hungry.

'The Drawing Pad'

Rossina had an idea, and had been almost overwhelmed with excitement when the City Art Gallery agreed to be approached for modestly funding her to achieve her goal.

The idea was that she would draw, and later paint in, every six months for five years the Scene of 'Leaving the Art Gallery'. She reckoned that there may still be Buses in five year's time, for example, but maybe fewer cars. She didn't know whether there would be more Tourists than presently in the Summer or fewer, or whether the Roman Bar to the town nearly opposite the Gallery would still have the newly placed figurines on the top of it or whether they would have been toppled off by then!

She would have hated to see the Bar all scrawled over by Graffiti, or even daubed with an edgy Banksy, but really also was not sure whether it would continue to be lit by fake-chain mail fairy lights every Wintertime or not.

She had to appear before a Panel, and the day of the Hearing made sure that she was smartly, though stylishly dressed. She wanted to make an impression that would be somewhat unforgettable without diving into eccentricity. In the end, she decided on a longer-than-usual skirt and a flowery neckerchief.

There were about six people on the Panel, which had met over a large glass table. The chairs seemed basic in a way, being wood-looking, but were massively more comfortable than most older wood chairs would have been, and were sculpted and curved to cause there to be no discomfort at all in not accepting fabric padding.

There were spotlights above, shining on them all not with the effect of intense scrutiny, but more with a modern hopeful feel that the City would not, in the space of five years only, descend into rack and ruin despite the Energy and Climate Change threat.

Some of the attendees had electronic devices to write into, but there was a lady there with paper and Parker Pen, and all had mobile phones evident which were hopefully still working.

The Scene made it certainly hopeful that she might succeed in getting a Commission.

Then, one of them started quizzing her about her own health. It had seemed unquestionable to her that she would succeed in being able to live and draw for the next five years, and she did not know whether to be insulted at the air of threat.

Further, one of them asked her how much Alcohol she consumed generally weekly, and whether Pregnancy was still a future consideration.

Rossina began to get upset at that. She became ruffled and prickly and even sarcastic in her manner in response to it: she could not help her temper fraying somewhat. She started countering by asking them whether they had any older Relatives that might need looking after soon. That was all met by a frosty silence.

Finally, the Panel asked her to leave them to arrive at their decision, and to wait in the seat in the adjoining room for a while.

Next, the lady who had had the Parker Pen approached her ten minutes later and told her that Unfortunately the Art Gallery had already had the same idea put to them by another Artist, so that she would have to leave the Panel further time to decide which of them would be granted the Commission.

Rossina was worried she might have to jump into the conclusion that actually the Council only wanted to steal ideas.

But then, two weeks later, she received a Telephone Call, which confirmed that the Panel had decided that it was indeed an excellent proposal and would be of interest both to Residents and Tourists.

'The Serenading Sparrows'

Martin was getting more and more certain that the local sparrows were keeping him in mind. At one point he had even reacted with anger and a degree of paranoia, but more recently he had begun to really believe that indeed, in reality, the sparrows were wanting his attention, purposely crowding round him, and gently coaxing him towards giving them his affection.

When he had been at the Paranoia stage of the lengthy courting by the birds he had even tried flying off to Paris, and there been met by a whole group of gently noisy birds that refused to be ignored.

He did not quite know what to do on any of the occasions. The birds were obviously wanting him to acknowledge their presence, and maybe even feed them some grain or broken off crumbs of bread from Local Bakeries, but he was conscious that if he fed them in Public he might automatically be regarded as some kind of eccentric vagrant and that he may even be reprimanded officially, or arrested for inciting bird-interest in Public Squares and venues.

He did not know whether it might be some kind of poking fun game by the chirpy characters, but was rather worried that they may genuinely need his help.

Was it some kind of Oscar Wilde Courtship by the Wildlife? Were they doing a 'Happy Prince' to him on purpose?

He had to avoid breaking down over the affair and continual attempts to break down his resistance, but could not avoid forming the belief that either someone had trained them somewhere to follow him and pester for his affection, or that something Supernatural was somehow occurring.

One time, in King's Square, a host of sweetly twirping Sparrows even braved all the potential Pigeons to pester for his attention as he observed a Piano Player and risked a Tomato and Cheese puff pastry square from the Bakery.

Certainly, he had to conclude, they had been more faithful companions than some of the women he had dated. They were seeming not to lose interest in him personally, even when he attempted to try and make them aware that he might have an intention to shirk them.

But lately there had been fewer of them. There was one particularly chirpy bird who he was beginning to think he could identify as an individual, who raised the volume of his tweeting louder than most of the others.

Who would have helped the poor and starving in 'The Happy Prince' if the sparrow had already been extinct?

'The Custom at Elf's Gate'

Mr Beacon bristled himself into order and began his Speech to the Assembly.

"In the Twenty-First Century at Elf's Gate it was always the Custom to counter any potential criticism or accusation with a Scientifically-sounding Counter-Offensive, either Medical or in fact Prejudicial Jargon, as long as it sounded Scientific or Professional: partly because it had been the case for some time that Organisations such as The Royal College of Psychiatrists had broken down entirely since none of the Councils could afford to pay Psychiatrists any longer and encouraged those without qualifications, in every field, those who had enough bluff capability to withstand the pressures of the deception, to try and nudge their own way into a regular income bracket via deception". He looked up from his Directory, hoping that he had caught the attention of the congregated Public gravely enough. It was now years and years ago, almost a Century ago since Dawkins was the main voice in charge of the Nation, when Oxford and Cambridge had roped him into colluding with their increasingly desperate attempts to keep the Economy afloat no matter how much morality might be forsaken by the exercise, no matter how many birds and bees and rodents wired-up in Labs suffered, and Chimpanzees squeezing themselves into the furiously passive acceptance of a banana in response to being tortured daily.

"If someone might be identified as a potential launcher of criticism, they were immediately said to have Learning Difficulties, with the idea being that it was not customary to launch any alternative perspective. If one didn't settle down in a Classroom immediately, even if one asked intelligent and relevant questions, the person was accused of being 'unable to concentrate' with the hope that they would be squeezed and crushed into both a state of humility and self-doubt, and that they would therefore become and indeed therefore be proved, ineffectual (particularly if it had ever been suspected that they might have wielded criticism). Any Public Lectures that took place were only allowed questioning by special bribes, to try and draw people into thinking that that particular University may be a good one, for example....and increasingly each Lecturer, in order to maintain his or her own personal wage, was pushed into refusing to accept questioning or challenging with more and more certainty, making the Educational process in fact not far from a Dumb Dictatorship.

" The few who took part in Public Debates were so worried that someone would be after them personally for having expressed a certain view, even if that view was expressed in a Rhetorical fashion and partly for effect and even Entertainment only, so worried that whole groups of people would want to force them into a situation wherein they would forever regret having said anything at all, that mostly they began to crave the quiet possibility of acting like animals who they had referred to formerly as 'dumb'.

"Meanwhile, however, it was generally the collusion to try and make out, particularly to younger Members at Elf's Gate, that the Country still generally backed Free Speech and Diversity of Belief and Opinion. Do any of you think that might really have been the case....?"

It was an old Video. That had been a newer Century ago again, and well before the new Planets had been inhabited by new examples of people who were the original Earth Citizens. Even when Mr Beacon had been alive though, Psychic forces had moved on so much further, once it had been proved in Dawkins time that Computers could read minds, and that Televisions could analyse viewers Thought-Processes. In the old Video, old-fashioned even for the time, in fact far out-dated given the newer Fairy precepts, everyone had seemed to prove that Mr Beacon might be wrong by not answering him...as though they were still themselves in the same state that he had described being the main problem a Century earlier.

But Dawson was not sure that any of the History existed in reality at all, nor whether he was a Lone Brain in a world that somehow was surviving only because it had shifted dimensions.

'Toby's Nightmare'

Toby was only eight years old, but he was seriously beginning to worry that even though it was now 2023 and the idea that the world had evolved and progressed had been so frequently stated, particularly by Mr Everington, his Head Master, particularly if he wanted to comfort them, or one of them had been bullied in the Playground....he might have to grow up to be a Pirate.

Earlier on, his Mother had frequently bought him books about Pirates, lovely coloured large-printed publications specially designed for children, and she'd even once bought him an entire Pirate outfit when he had attended Jake's Birthday Dressing-Up Party. There had been balloons and goody-bags afterwards then, as well, and even a Magician in the Marquee in the Garden. There had been Ham Sandwiches and Cream Cakes, and the Adults had had Earl Grey Tea from delicate flower-printed China cups, poised on matching saucers, all with golden rims. There had been a Hammock, proper string, all set up by the Willow Tree, and a Masked Paper-Mache shape for them all to take turns at beating with a rod, until finally it gave up hundreds of sweets, scattered all over the grass, some half-hidden by the daisies that the Lawnmower had somehow missed or found too tough for it.

There had been a Full-Sized Record Player and a stack of about 200 Records all waiting-to-be-available for them, and the Samantha woman had been recruited to do the Face-Painting, and then later on there had been a Karaoke Machine on a long long extension lead brought specially for them to Sing Loudly and Confidently into.

But that had been earlier on.

'The Walk by the River'

Matthew could hardly believe how lovely it was outside, having been cooped-up for three years with a condition that took him in and out of Hospital regularly, over which his Mother fussed so obsessively that she could hardly leave the medicine cupboard unattended even for more than a quarter of an hour, after so much waiting in the car as she collected new prescriptions for him from the Chemist, and after so much anxiety that he might die.

He had definitely improved immensely. All the obsessing had, in fact, in his particular case, been worth it...and the future ahead, as long as the weather permitted and his Dad kept his Job, would hopefully now be a long and happy one.

It was so good to get some fresh air after the sterility of his confinement in his bedroom, and though he had feared his legs might have got so weak, and his back so unused to being asked to pull the nerves needed to manipulate him, he had found, though he was admittedly a bit trembly, that he could not only balance, but even negotiate tufts of grass and the occasional danger of turned-over stones in the walk-way.

He could hardly believe all this had been round the corner, only ten minutes away from his house, for all that time he had been confined. People passing and smiling with dogs which were friendly, and even ducks still quacking nearer the reeds in the River itself.

There were Blackberries ripening in the hedgerows, and still an occasional butterfly flitting past and up and across.

He wanted to sit down by the side of the path and play with the sticks, proper, wooden sticks, that he had gathered from by-the-side of the wooded area earlier on. He really wanted to stay there as long as he could before Teatime, and feel the basking of the sweet sunshine on his face.

Flowers danced in the slight breeze, pink ones and white ones, Campions Florence said.

He was ever-so-joyous to be out-and-about and alive and well.

The Old Teddy Bear

Julie could hardly believe it when her old Teddy Bear, her Teddy Bear from when she had last been about twelve years old, turned up in her Flat in her Fifties. It was making out, had been making out, that it had been hiding all the time in the back of the wardrobe, but she knew for certain that some Magic must have planted it there, or some Intruder or Ghost of a Relative. She did not quite know how to take it, but she couldn't deny that she was happy to see it again.

Teddy Edwards, it had been called, though it wore a lovely knitted lace dress that she had taken off her earlier doll. She had felt that Edward really needed clothing as somehow he looked so bare before she had put it on him for keeps. It was suspected that the Dress had originally been knitted for her own self, when she had been only a baby, but it suited Teddy Edward marvellously and she loved him for being more decently charming that way than most Teddies in the Universe.

She thought it had probably been her Nanna who had knitted it: and very few people now would have been able to knit that way and make it so neat and fine and full of complicated stitchery. But though it was intricate it was not at all transparent, and it had always been tough enough to survive the few times that she had had to take it off to wash it.

It crossed her mind that it might be Alien Psychologists who had somehow placed him back with her, and though she felt a bit fuzzled by that thought the sight of his blue eyes and lamb-like fur was so overwhelmingly charming …she was still so marvellously fond of him, that she was not discomfited enough to speculate about any of it much further.

If she had told Alan, he might have said that somehow she was suffering from some form of Dementia, but she would never have believed him because here he was, in reality, in physical person....her own exactly preserved Teddy Edwards.

Printed in Great Britain
by Amazon